Pi[illegible]use
Where Are You?

By Alison Green
Illustrated by Deborah Allwright

4
3
2
1

Pinkie Mouse and Pangolin
were playing hide-and-squeak.
Pangolin had shut his eyes
and promised not to peek.

Now pangolins are sensible,
they don't like being brave,
And Pangolin remembered
all the **warnings** Daddy gave:

"Don't hide-and-squeak near busy **bees**!
They'll hurt you when they sting.
Don't hide-and-squeak near **chimpanzees**!
They'll bash you when they swing.

"Don't hide-and-squeak near **elephants**!
Don't hide behind their poo!
They'll stomp you without meaning to,
and bruise you black and blue."

But Pinkie Mouse was naughty.
She had mischief in her head.
So Pangolin went seeking
and ignored what Daddy said.

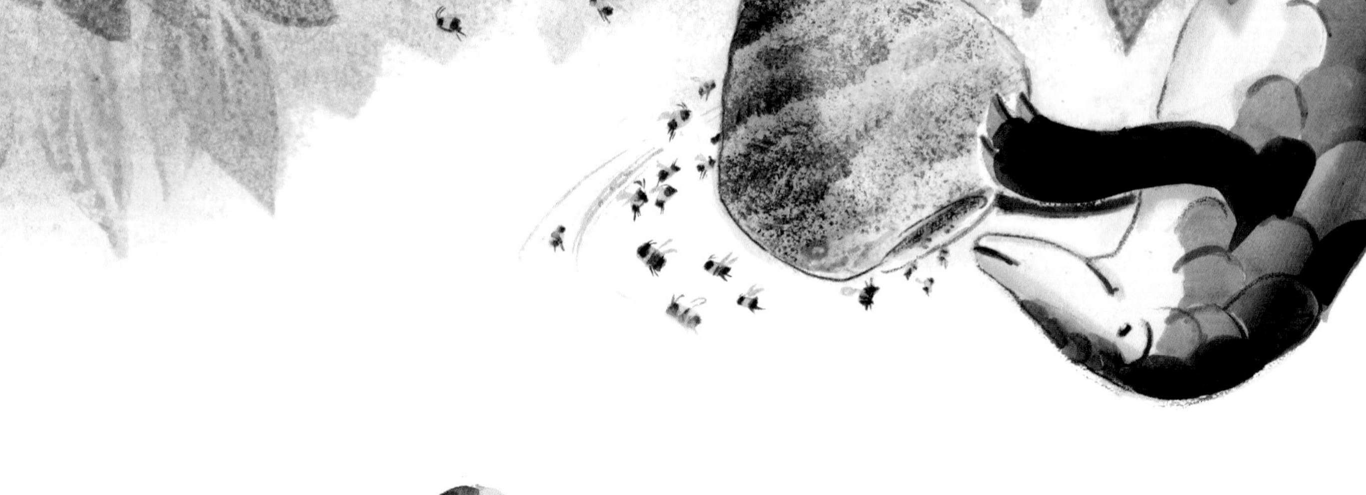

He sniffed around the bees' nest
but the bees all made him sneeze.

He tried to ask directions from
a troupe of chimpanzees.

He crept along a creeper (which is very hard to do.)

Then he tiptoed round an elephant,
and checked behind her poo.

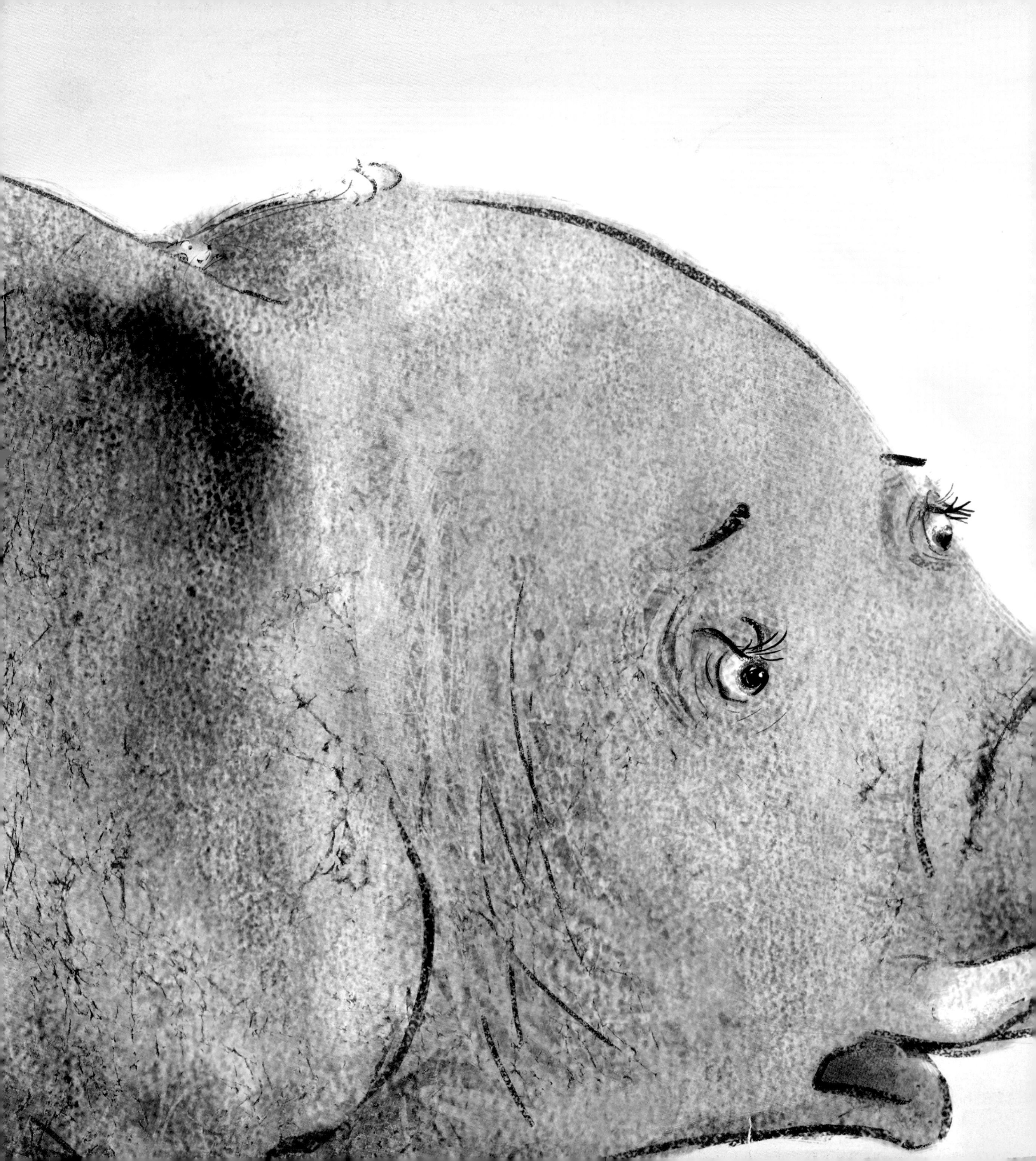

"Excuse me!" said the elephant. "I've never seen such cheek!
A lady's poo is **not** the place to play at hide-and-squeak!"

"Oh, Pinkie Mouse, stop hiding, it's not funny any more.
This elephant's quite angry and my tail is getting sore!"

Now pangolins are rather shy,
they just hate being brave,
And Pangolin remembered
all the **warnings** Mummy gave:

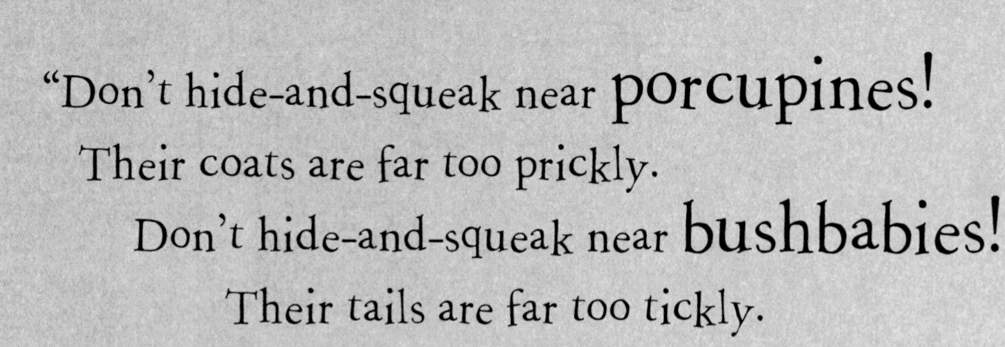

"Don't hide-and-squeak near **porcupines!**
Their coats are far too prickly.
Don't hide-and-squeak near **bushbabies!**
Their tails are far too tickly.

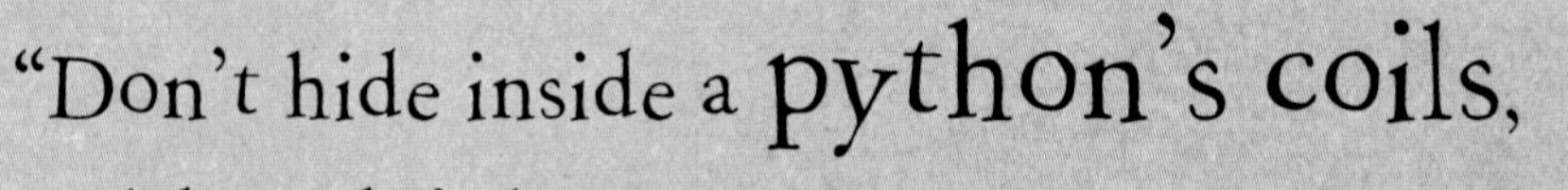

"Don't hide inside a **python's coils**,
although it looks so easy.
They'll squish and squeeze you, just to tease you,
till you're feeling queasy."

But Pinkie wouldn't do what's right,
She'd do what's brave instead.
So Pangolin went seeking,
and ignored what Mummy said.

He snuffled round some bushbabies,
which tickled till he shrieked.
He peered beneath a porcupine
which prickled till he squeaked.

He crept up to a python
while it watched him, glinty-eyed,
Then bravely climbed its coils
to see if Pinkie was inside.

"Excuse me, Mr Python,
but I'm playing hide-and-squeak!
Could you, perhaps, not **squeeze** so much?
It's getting hard to speak."

"Forgive me," hissed the python,
"but I'm feeling **super-squeezy!**"
"That's funny," sniffled Pangolin.
"**I'm** feeling super-**sneezy** . . ."

"A-tish-a-woo!"

went Pangolin – his biggest ever sneeze.
It blew him out of Python's coils and up some mango trees.
"Oh, please stop hiding, Pinkie Mouse, I'm getting quite fed up.
I'm bashed and bruised. I need a snooze. I'm ready to give up!"

Now, pangolins aren't brave, but they will never leave their friends.
So Pangolin walked on and on to where the wide world ends.
At last he searched some rushes by the slimy-grimy Nile . . .

And almost slipped inside the jaws of

Mr Crocodile!

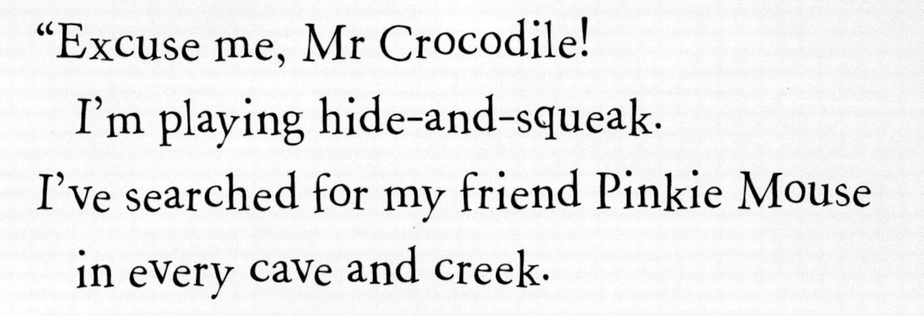

"Excuse me, Mr Crocodile!
I'm playing hide-and-squeak.
I've searched for my friend Pinkie Mouse
in every cave and creek.

"I've simply got to find her,
but she's brave as brave can be,
So I'm doing all the scary things
she'd do if she were me."

"A tragic tale," said Crocodile.
"Now, let me think awhile . . .
I think she may be hiding
deep inside my croco-smile.

"Do step inside and look around,
I'd be most gratified.
It really is the perfect place
for any mouse to hide."

Now, pangolins are timid,
they would rather stay in bed.
And Pangolin remembered
what his granny always said:

"Don't hide-and-squeak in **crocodiles**!
They'll eat you as a snack."
"But I have to look!" said Pangolin.
"I really can't turn back."

The croco-smile was full of teeth.
He didn't want to go.

He plucked up all his courage –
then a tiny voice cried . . .

"No!!!"

"It's Pinkie Mouse! Oh, Pinkie,
I've been looking everywhere!"
"I called to you," cried Pinkie.
"But you never saw me there.

"My voice was just too squeaky,
I could never make you hear.
My legs were far too little,
I could never quite get near.

"But I watched you, and I saw
how many brave things you can do.
I really hope that when I'm big
I'll be as brave as you!"

Pinkie Mouse and Pangolin
were playing hide-and-squeak.

3

2

1

Pinkie Mouse went, "Three, two, one!"
and scampered off to seek.

She found her friend – it wasn't hard.
His snores were loud and deep.
His eyes were shut, his tail was curled –
he'd fallen fast asleep.

ZZZ
ZZZ

what are pangolins?

You've probably never met a pangolin. They live in the tropical parts of Asia and Africa, and they're very, very shy. They sleep all day, curled up in a little ball, and only come out at night.

Photograph © 2009 Valerius Tygart

super scales

Pangolins are also called 'scaly anteaters', because they're covered in big scales, to protect them from other animals. The scales are made from the same substance as our fingernails and hair, but they're really strong. When pangolins are scared, they quickly roll into a ball so that all their scales stick out like a hedgehog's prickles.

super scaly!

ants for breakfast, lunch and dinner!

Pangolins are called anteaters because they eat . . . ants! (And other insects called termites.) They slurp them up with their long, sticky tongues, and one small pangolin can eat about 70 million insects a year. Yummy!

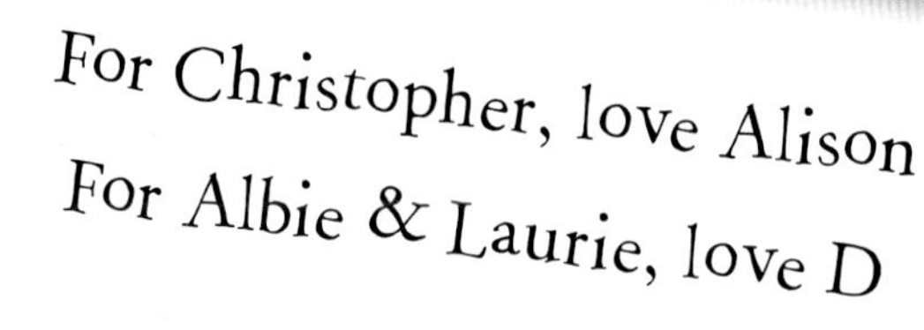

For Christopher, love Alison

For Albie & Laurie, love D

First published in 2011 by Alison Green Books
An imprint of Scholastic Children's Books
Euston House, 24 Eversholt Street, London NW1 1DB
A division of Scholastic Ltd
www.scholastic.co.uk
London - New York - Toronto - Sydney - Auckland - Mexico City - New Delhi - Hong Kong

HB ISBN: 978 1 407110 67 7 / PB ISBN: 978 1 407110 68 4
 Printed in Singapore

10 9 8 7 6 5 4 3 2 1

Papers used by Scholastic Children's Books are made from wood grown in sustainable forests.

A Note to Grown-ups

Sadly, Pangolins are currently endangered, but lots of groups are working to make sure they are protected. If you want to find out more about pangolins, visit: www.savepangolins.org.